Paddington's Cookery Book

"I bet it's got marmalade in it," said Jonathan.
"Paddington's things always have marmalade."
Paddington Abroad

For more Paddington books, activities, games and fun visit:
www.paddingtonbear.com

First published in hardback by HarperCollins Children's Books in 2011

1 3 5 7 9 10 8 6 4 2

ISBN: 978-0-00-742367-5

HarperCollins Children's Books is a division of HarperCollins Publishers Ltd.

Recipes by Lesley Young
Photography by Laura Ashman
Page 38 photo (nettles) used under licence from Shutterstock
Food prepared by Peter McCall

Visit our website at: www.harpercollins.co.uk

Printed and bound in China

MICHAEL BOND

Paddington's Cookery Book

Recipes by Lesley Young
Illustrated by R.W. Alley

HarperCollins *Children's Books*

Safety in the Kitchen

Mrs Bird is in charge of the Browns' kitchen at number 32 Windsor Gardens and she runs what Mr Brown calls a tight ship. Although she is always grateful when anyone offers to help, she has a strict set of rules:

1. Before starting work, wash your hands or paws thoroughly.

2. Children must always have a grown-up to help them – essential when they are using a sharp knife, handling anything hot or using a food processor.

3. Make sure all pot handles point towards the wall in case you knock into them by mistake and spill the contents.

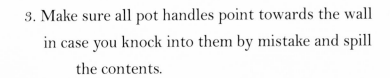

4. Never leave frying pans or saucepans on the heat unattended.

5. Always wear oven gloves when you are putting things in and taking things out of the oven.

Contents

Introduction
by Michael Bond

A great many books have been written about food, and it would be a very lowly bookshop indeed that didn't have a section devoted to the subject. Most of them have been written by chefs, which is not so surprising. They come and go like the weather.

But one of the longest lasting of all time is the work of a French lawyer who never went near a stove in his life if he could possibly help it, and yet he ended up having a cheese named after him as a token of respect. He achieved worldwide fame and it is even said he introduced scrambled eggs to America when he fled there during the French Revolution.

His name was Jean Anthelme Brillat-Savarin, and his most famous book, *The Physiology of Taste*, was published in December 1825, two months before he died.

He was a master of the quotable phrase, and one of my favourites is, "Tell me what you eat, and I will tell you what you are."

I often wonder what conclusions he would have reached had he come across one of Paddington's marmalade sandwiches.

"A strong sense of right and wrong; well meaning, but accident-prone; drives a hard bargain; has a liking for anything new, but is careful with his money; one of nature's bachelors; fond of marmalade; painstaking…"

I say that because Monsieur Brillat-Savarin never married and he was satisfied with the simplest of dishes, provided they were made with style. He would have been most impressed by the way Paddington arranges his chunks. Like his old bush hat, it is a gift that has been handed down and is not given to many.

Michael Bond
London

Foreword
by Paddington

When I read Michael Bond's introduction telling how someone called Mr Brillat-Savarin had a cheese named after him, I couldn't help wondering which kind of cheese might go with my name. It kept me awake several nights running. Then my best friend, Mr Gruber, brought me back down to earth.

"First of all, Mr Brown," he said, "you will need to write a book. Mind you," he added, "you never know what you can do until you try."

He went on to point out that eating isn't simply a matter of keeping body and soul together. "A lot of people aren't lucky enough to have three meals a day," he said. "But if they are, it adds up to over a thousand meals each year of their life, so it is only sensible to make sure they enjoy them, otherwise it is a terrible waste."

And then, much to my surprise, Mrs Bird offered to give me cookery lessons. (I think Mr Gruber may have had a word with her on the quiet.)

First of all she found a special wooden box for me to stand on, and then she gave me one of her old aprons to wear in case I got stains on my duffle coat.

And because she has strong views on the old argument as to which came first – the chicken or the egg – she suggested we start with eggs. Mrs Bird is very keen on eggs. She thinks they are the most useful item of food in anyone's larder.

It just so happened that only the other day I had been reading about a town in France called Bessières. Every year they celebrate Easter by making an omelette from more than 12,000 eggs. It sounded a very good idea.

Mrs Bird gave one of her snorts. "They would," she said. "But in cooking you must learn to walk before you can run. Besides, I don't have a big enough pan for that kind of thing."

"They have one which is over four metres wide," I said. "It fills the town square."

"Well, there you are," said Mrs Bird. "But we are not talking about making an omelette. I grant you trying to scramble one egg is a waste of time, so we will start off with two, which isn't as easy as it might sound."

Breakfast

Omelettes come in various sizes, but among the biggest ever must be one that was made in France for Napoleon Bonaparte.

The Emperor was leading his army back to Paris from the south of France when they stopped in Bessières for a night's rest. The next morning he so enjoyed an omelette he was given for breakfast that he ordered the innkeeper to make one large enough to feed his whole army, and the event has been celebrated annually ever since.

It brings it all to life. I can see now why Mrs Bird wouldn't want one that size in her kitchen.

Scrambled Eggs

Serves 1

You will need:

bowl

fork

non-stick frying pan

knife

wooden spoon

Ingredients:

2 large fresh eggs

salt and pepper

25g (1oz) butter

What to do:

- Break the eggs into the bowl. Add a pinch of salt and some freshly ground pepper.

- Whisk with the fork for just a minute to break up the yolks and whites.

- Put the pan on a medium heat. When it is hot, add about two-thirds of the butter and swirl it round until it is melted and just on the point of foaming.

- Add the eggs. Stir with the wooden spoon – round the sides and into the middle – until the eggs form fat, soft curds and are almost cooked.

- Now take the pan off the heat, add the rest of the butter, and keep stirring. The eggs will continue to cook in the heat from the pan, but will not be dry and overcooked.

- Season with salt and pepper and serve at once on hot, buttered toast.

MRS BIRD'S TIP: Make sure the heat is evenly distributed to the mixture at all times and don't be in too much of a hurry.

Marmalade

Mrs Bird always says if you don't follow the instructions in a recipe you only have yourself to blame if it doesn't work, so make sure you read the list of ingredients carefully or, as in my case… *listen*.

I say that because when I offered to do the shopping for Mrs Bird I thought she wanted several oranges, but it turned out she said "Seville" oranges. They come from Spain and are especially good for making marmalade. Unfortunately, they are only in the shops for a short spell towards the end of winter and there is always a big rush for them, so we nearly went without that year.

I often find thick chunks come in useful. Like the time Mr Gruber and I went round the maze at Hampton Court. I left a trail of them on the bushes, so we found our way out again in record time. The man in charge was so surprised I thought he was going to give Mr Gruber his money back. He didn't, of course. I should have given him one of my hard stares!

To add a personal touch: Get some plain, gummed labels and write "Marmalade" on them, along with the date. When I help I usually add my mark to show it was made entirely by paw. P.B.

You will need:

small plate

saucepan large enough to hold 1kg (2lb 4oz) oranges and 2½ litres (4½ pints) of water

sharp knife

chopping board

large spoon

lemon squeezer

wooden spoon

ladle

small square of muslin, with string to tie it shut

clean screw-top jars

waxed paper circles

MRS BIRD'S TIP:
It's best to have as many jars as possible ready and waiting. Too few and you will have a problem on your hands.

What to do:

• Put a small plate in the fridge.

• Wash the oranges and place them in the saucepan with 2½ litres (4½ pints) of water.

• Bring to the boil, then simmer until the skins are soft.

• Lower the heat and remove the oranges with the large spoon. When they are cool enough to handle, cut them in half.

• Remove the orange pips and put them in the muslin square, tying it shut with the string.

• Squeeze all the juice from the oranges and add it to the saucepan of water.

• Slice the peel into strips as thin or thick as you want.

• Add the peel to the saucepan along with the bag of pips (they contain pectin, which helps the marmalade set), note the level of the water, and turn up the heat again until it boils.

• Leave the mixture to boil gently for an hour or so, until the contents have been reduced by about a third. After the first half hour preheat the oven to 180°C (350°F/Gas mark 4), ready for the jars.

• Remove the bag of pips. Pour in the sugar and bring to the boil again. Squeeze the lemon and add the juice to the saucepan (this will make the marmalade sparkle and help it to set).

• Stir the mixture until all the sugar is dissolved, then leave it to simmer.

Ingredients:

1kg (2lb 4oz) Seville oranges, clean and free of blemishes, with thick, soft skins

1 lemon

2kg (4½lbs) granulated sugar

- Wait until the mixture begins to darken.

- In the meantime, sterilise the jars by washing them thoroughly in warm, soapy water. Rinse and dry them and put them in the warm oven.

- Test whether the marmalade has reached setting point by putting a small spoonful on to the cold plate from the fridge. Leave for a moment or two before poking it with your finger. The surface should wrinkle.

- Remove the jars from the oven and use the ladle to fill them with marmalade.

- As soon as each jar is full, place a paper disc on top and leave to cool. Then screw the tops on.

I find pouring it through a funnel makes less mess. Mrs Bird bought me one soon after Mr Brown got stuck to the kitchen floor one year. P. B.

Smoothies

After a hard morning at the stove there is nothing like a smoothie.

Serves 1-2

You will need:

chopping board

sharp knife

measuring jug

tablespoon

juice squeezer

blender or liquidiser

ice cubes

What to do:

- For each drink measure out the ingredients, put them in the blender or liquidiser, add a few ice cubes, and process until they are glossily smooth.

If you stop too soon you might end up with LUMPIES, like I did. P. B.

Tropical Pineapple

Ingredients:

1 small, ripe pineapple, peeled, cored and chopped

1 ripe banana, peeled and chopped

2 tbsp coconut cream

1 tbsp runny honey

squeeze of lime juice

Strawberry Bounce

Ingredients:

300ml (10 fl oz) apple juice

100ml (3½fl oz) natural yogurt

1 ripe banana, peeled and chopped

200g (7oz) strawberries

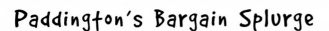

Paddington's Bargain Splurge

When the traders in the Portobello Market are clearing up at the end of the day they are often only too pleased to accept offers for any left-overs.

Unfortunately there are a lot of other things they are happy to get rid of besides and Mrs Bird has to put my shopping basket on wheels outside because they start to smell.

Serves 2-4

Ingredients:

1 large, ripe mango, peeled and stoned

1 small, ripe melon (or ½ a large one), peeled, seeded and chopped

150ml (¼ pint) orange juice

1 small punnet ripe raspberries

That's just one example... and it only costs sixpence! P. B.

Blueberry Muffins

Makes 12 muffins

You will need:

mixing bowl

another bowl

sieve

measuring jug

whisk

teaspoon

large metal spoon

tablespoon

muffin tray lined with 12 paper cases

What to do:

- Preheat oven to 180°C (350°F/Gas mark 4).

- Put the sugar in the mixing bowl. Sift the flour and baking powder on top.

- In the other bowl, whisk the milk, eggs, oil and vanilla extract together until smooth.

- With the whisk, make a well in the centre of the flour mixture and beat in the liquid mixture, quickly and roughly. Don't worry about the odd lump – speed keeps the air in and makes the muffins light.

Ingredients:

125g (4½oz) caster sugar

200g (7oz) plain flour

2 tsp baking powder

175ml (6fl oz) milk

2 eggs

150ml (¼ pint) vegetable oil

1tsp vanilla extract

200g (7oz) blueberries

- Quickly fold in the blueberries with the large metal spoon.

- With the tablespoon, place the mixture into the muffin cases.

- Bake for 30 minutes, until golden brown and risen.

I couldn't help licking my lips when Mrs Bird took the muffins out of the oven.

"You can try one when they've cooled down," she said. "But good chefs get their pleasure from seeing others enjoy the fruits of their labour."

I did as I was told, but I couldn't help thinking I might not make a very good chef.

Elevenses

Real Hot Chocolate

Most mornings I visit my best friend, Mr Gruber, at his antique shop in the Portobello Market. I call in at a bakers on the way, where I have a standing order for buns, and Mr Gruber supplies the cocoa, which he makes on a stove at the back of his shop. Then we have our elevenses together while we discuss things in general.

Luckily we share the same tastes. I like my buns plain, and Mr Gruber likes his cocoa as it comes; straight from the packet.

But once in a while, if it is a special occasion, or he has had a successful week in his shop, he says the magic words, "I'm going to push the boat out now, Mr Brown," and we have real hot chocolate.

Serves 2

You will need:

2 mugs

chopping board

sharp knife or grater

tablespoon

medium saucepan

2 bowls (one of them heatproof)

whisk

Ingredients:

1½ mugs of whole milk

100g (3½oz) chocolate (dark or milk)

50ml (1¾fl oz) whipping cream

What to do:

- Chop the chocolate finely, or grate it. Set aside 2 tablespoons for later and put the rest in the heatproof bowl.

- Whip the cream until soft peaks form.

- Put the milk in the saucepan and heat until it's hot but not boiling.

- Pour the milk over the chocolate and whisk until it's melted.

- Pour into the mugs. Float the whipped cream on top and sprinkle the rest of the chocolate over it.

Then we sit back and hope no customers come in! P. B.

Iced Buns

Mrs Bird says the simplest things to cook are often the hardest to get right, and buns are a good example. No two are ever exactly the same – even if they come from the same baker. So she suggested I might like to try my paw at making a very different sort to my usual.

Makes 12 buns

You will need:

small saucepan

wooden spoon

measuring jug

large bowl

tablespoon

teaspoon

round-bladed knife

clingfilm

large baking sheet

wire cooling rack

small bowl

What to do:

- Put the sultanas and cinnamon in the saucepan, pour over the orange juice and bring to a simmer. Take off the heat and set aside to cool. (The sultanas will absorb the juice and plump up.)

- Put the flour, yeast and sugar into the large bowl. Make a well in the centre with a tablespoon and break in the egg.

- Melt the butter and add it to the bowl, along with 100ml (3½ fl oz) tepid water.

- Bring this all together with the knife, until it starts to make a soft dough. Turn it out on to a floured surface. Knead for 10 minutes or so until the dough is smooth and elastic.

- Add the sultanas and knead again for a couple of minutes. Put the dough back in the clean bowl, cover with clingfilm and leave in a warm place, like an airing cupboard, for an hour and a half, until doubled in size.

Ingredients:

150g (5oz) sultanas

1 tsp cinnamon

4tbsp orange juice

350g (12oz) strong white bread flour

7g (¼oz) sachet instant dried yeast

25g (1oz) caster sugar

1 medium egg

100g (3½oz) unsalted butter

a little oil, for greasing

200g (7oz) icing sugar

tepid water (from the kettle)

- Turn the dough out on to the floured surface again, and knock out any air by giving it a good punch.

- Cut into 12 evenly-sized bits, shape into fat sausages and put on the greased baking sheet, spacing them well apart.

- Cover loosely with some oiled clingfilm and leave to rest for another hour and a half, until doubled in size again. While this is happening, preheat the oven to 180°C (350°F/Gas mark 4).

- Bake for 15 minutes, until they are golden brown.

- Put them on the wire rack to cool.

- Mix the icing sugar in the small bowl with a little water until you get the right consistency: not too thick or too thin.

- Ice the buns with the knife and leave to set.

(There should be twelve unless you couldn't wait. P. B.)

"That's very strange," said Mrs Bird, when she put the buns out to cool. "I could have sworn there were twelve."

(I couldn't wait! P. B.)

Croque Monsieur

The first thing Mrs Bird gave me to cook all by myself was a croque monsieur. It's a French dish, and she said it would be a good test of how good I was at laying everything out before I started.

Serves 2

You will need:

cheese grater

chopping board

knife for buttering

small saucepan

tablespoon

wooden spoon

frying pan

fish slice

What to do:

• Grate the cheese.

• Butter the bread, using 20g (¾oz) or a third of the block of butter, and put the slices on a board, buttered sides down.

• Melt the rest of the butter in the saucepan over a medium heat and add the flour. Stir with the wooden spoon for a couple of minutes until well mixed, then add the milk gradually, stirring all the time, until the mixture is thick and smooth.

Ingredients:

75g (3oz) Gruyère cheese

60g (2½oz) butter, softened

4 thick slices white bread

15g (½oz) plain flour

100ml (3½fl oz) whole milk

1 egg yolk

1 tablespoon Dijon mustard

4 slices good quality ham

- Take the saucepan off the heat and stir in the egg yolk, the mustard and the grated cheese. Beat the sauce with the spoon until the cheese has melted.

- Spread the cheese mixture on 2 slices of the bread waiting on the board. Fold the ham and put 2 pieces on top of each of the cheese-sauce-covered slices. Put the remaining 2 slices of bread on top of each of the cheese and ham slices (butter side up) and press down softly.

- Heat a frying pan over a medium heat and cook the sandwiches for about 3 minutes on each side until they are crisp and golden. (Because they are buttered, you don't need any fat or oil.)

- Using the fish slice, take them out of the pan, cut into halves diagonally, and serve at once.

Mine didn't turn out quite as I had hoped, but Mrs Bird was very good about it. She said it could happen to anyone and that perhaps another time we should add a fire extinguisher to the list of things that are needed. Anyway, it was a lesson in what can go wrong in a kitchen.

We cut the one we had left over into two and she pronounced it, "As good as they come," which was praise indeed.

Portobello Road

I have lost track of how long it is since I first arrived in Britain and the Browns made me part of their family, but during that time all manner of strange ingredients have started to appear on the vegetable stalls in the Portobello Road.

At first they were mostly bought by people of various nationalities who, like me, have made Britain their home, but Mr Gruber says that, variety being the spice of life, we should be grateful. They have made a big contribution to British tastes as well and people have become much more adventurous in what they eat.

The following are a few you might like to try. Falafels, for instance, are very popular in the Middle East and they can be served in lots of different ways; as a sandwich filler along with lettuce and tomatoes, or in the form of a hamburger.

falafels

Serves 2-4

You will need:

bowl

colander

food processor

chopping board

sharp knife

teaspoon

tablespoon

spatula

juice squeezer

*wide, shallow pan
(or frying pan)*

slotted spoon

kitchen paper

Ingredients:

*225g (8oz) dried
chickpeas*

1 garlic clove, crushed

1 tsp ground cumin

1 tsp ground coriander

*good pinch cayenne
pepper*

2 tbsp chopped parsley

juice of ½ lemon

1 tsp baking powder

vegetable oil, for frying

What to do:

• Put the chickpeas in the bowl, cover with cold water and soak overnight.

• Drain, and put in the food processor with all the other ingredients.

• Whizz until everything is smoothly mixed.

• Scrape out of the processor into a bowl. If you can, leave in the fridge for a couple of hours for the flavours to develop.

• Shape the mixture into small balls. Flatten them slightly. Put oil in the pan, to a depth of about 3cm (1in). Heat until the oil is hot enough to turn a small cube of bread golden and crispy.

• Fry the falafels until they are golden and cooked through – about 3 minutes on each side.

• Remove with a slotted spoon and drain on kitchen paper.

Roasted Pumpkin Soup

Serves 4-6

You will need:

chopping board

sharp knife

large bowl

roasting tin

fish slice

large saucepan

medium saucepan

wooden spoon

wand blender (or liquidiser)

cheese grater

Ingredients:

1 small pumpkin, about 1kg (2lb 4oz)

150ml (¼ pint) olive oil

2 garlic cloves, chopped

good pinch dried red chilli flakes

salt and pepper

2 tbsp olive oil

2 shallots (or 1 medium onion)

1 litre (1¾ pints) chicken stock

extra olive oil

grated Parmesan cheese, for serving

What to do:

- Preheat the oven to 200°C (400°F/Gas mark 6).

- Peel the pumpkin and cut into thin wedges – about 3cm (1in) thick.

- Put in the bowl with the oil, garlic and chilli, and mix to coat the wedges well. Tip out on to the roasting tin and roast in the oven for about 45 minutes, turning a couple of times with the fish slice, until soft and browned at the edges.

- Heat the stock in the medium saucepan. Chop the shallots or onion. Heat 2 tablespoons of olive oil in the large saucepan over a medium heat, add the shallots or onion, stir well and cook until soft. Tip in the pumpkin and stir for a minute or so. Pour on the stock, bring to a simmer and cook for 10 minutes. Now whizz everything with a wand blender or, in batches, in a liquidiser. Add salt and pepper to taste.

- Serve drizzled with a little olive oil and with a good sprinkling of grated Parmesan.

Roasted Pumpkin and Couscous Salad

Serves 4-6

You will need:

large heatproof bowl

lemon squeezer

wooden spoon

fork

tablespoon

Ingredients:

275g (10oz) couscous

500ml (18fl oz) vegetable stock, hot

3 tbsps olive oil

1 small pumpkin, roasted

juice of 1 lemon

chopped parsley

salt and pepper

feta cheese (optional)

1 pomegranate (optional)

What to do:

- Put the couscous in a large heatproof bowl and cover with the hot vegetable stock and a generous slick of olive oil. Leave for 10 minutes. Break up with a fork and add the roast pumpkin (see p28), the juice of a lemon, some chopped parsley, a couple of tablespoons more olive oil, and salt and pepper to taste.

- Crumbled feta cheese is good added to this. To make it extra special, scatter pomegranate seeds on top; cut the pomegranate in half and, holding a half over the salad, hit it hard with a wooden spoon to make the seeds rain down. The ruby bright seeds look wonderful with the orange pumpkin.

Stuffed Baked Potatoes

Peru is the original home of potatoes. They were an important part of the diet long before the rest of the world knew about them. According to Mr Gruber, the oldest potato on record was found in a cave in the Chilca Canyon region of Darkest Peru. It had been there since 8,000 BC! I expect it was too old to use by then.

Mrs Bird would have taken it back. P.B.

Serves 4

You will need:

baking tray

fork

chopping board

sharp knife

tablespoon

mixing bowl

potato masher

cheese grater

Ingredients:

4 large baking potatoes

50g (2oz) butter

4 tbsp milk

100g (3½oz) Cheddar cheese

salt and pepper

What to do:

- Preheat oven to 200°C (400°F/Gas mark 6).

- Lightly grease the baking tray.

- Scrub and dry the potatoes and prick them all over with the fork.

- Put them on the baking tray and bake in the oven for 1½ hours.

- Take the tray out, cut each potato in half lengthwise and carefully scoop the insides out into the mixing bowl.

- Put the 8 potato skin shells back on to the baking tray.

- Mash the potatoes with the butter and milk until they're smooth and creamy.

- Grate the cheese and add 75g (3oz) to the mashed potato, with salt and pepper to taste.

- Spoon the mixture into the potato shells. Sprinkle the rest of the cheese over them.

- Put back in the oven for about 30 minutes to heat through and brown.

Sweetcorn fritters

Serves 2-4

You will need:

large bowl

sieve

kitchen roll

measuring jug

tablespoon

whisk (hand or electric)

frying pan

fish slice

Ingredients:

100g (3½oz) plain flour

1 tbsp baking powder

salt and pepper

1 large egg

150ml (¼ pint) milk

200g (7oz) tinned sweetcorn kernels

2 tbsp vegetable oil

What to do:

• Sift the flour, baking powder and a good pinch of salt and pepper into the bowl. Make a well in the centre, add the egg and gradually beat in the milk with a whisk to form a smooth batter.

• Drain the sweetcorn kernels thoroughly. (Patting with kitchen roll is a good idea – it stops extra liquid diluting the batter.) Add the kernels to the batter mix.

• Heat the vegetable oil in the frying pan over a medium heat. Fry dollops (about 2 tablespoons) of the mixture for 2 minutes or so on each side until golden and crisp.

Guacamole

Serves 2-4

You will need:

chopping board

sharp knife

heatproof bowl

mixing bowl

slotted spoon

teaspoon

fork

tablespoon

serving bowl

clingfilm or foil

Ingredients:

2 ripe avocados

2 large ripe tomatoes

½ red onion

juice of 1 lime

1 small green or red chilli

2 tbsp fresh coriander

salt and pepper

What to do:

- Put the tomatoes in a heatproof bowl and cover with boiling water. Leave for 1 minute. Take them out with a slotted spoon, and put in a bowl of cold water to cool.

- Peel off the skins. Cut the tomatoes in half, scoop out the seeds with a teaspoon and discard them.

- Cut the avocados in half, remove the stones and peel. Chop the flesh and put it in the serving bowl. Mash with the fork. Pour over the lime juice, stirring it with the tablespoon to mix well. Chop the tomatoes and red onion finely. Add them to the bowl and mix through.

- Slit the chilli, scrape out the seeds and discard. Chop the chilli finely and mix in well. (Always wash your hands well after handling chillies.) Chop the coriander finely and add it to the bowl, stirring everything well. Add salt and pepper to taste.

- Cover the bowl with clingfilm or foil and put in the fridge for an hour or so before serving.

33

Aunt Lucy's Corner

I have been keeping my Aunt Lucy up to date with all my cooking activities by means of postcards and in return she has sent me some Peruvian recipes.

Sweet Potato Mash

This recipe is very popular with the inhabitants of the Home for Retired Bears in Lima. It goes with practically any hot dish, and given its colour it is especially popular with those who won't eat their greens. (Like some English boys I could mention, when they were small – or so I'm told. "No names – no pack drill!" as Mr Gruber would say.)

Serves 4-6

You will need:

large saucepan

colander

chopping board

small sharp knife

potato masher

tablespoon

Ingredients:

1kg (2lb 4oz) sweet potatoes

2 tbsp honey

juice of 1 orange

25g (1oz) butter

salt and pepper

What to do:

- Put the sweet potatoes in the saucepan and cover them with water.

- Bring to the boil, turn down the heat and simmer for about 20 minutes, or until soft.

- Drain the sweet potatoes and leave until they are cool enough to handle. With the small knife, peel off the skins.

- Chop the sweet potatoes roughly and put back in the saucepan. Add the butter and mash well. Now add the honey and the orange juice.

- Put the pan back on a low to medium heat and beat well with the wooden spoon until heated through and smooth.

- Season with salt and pepper.

Frozen Limonada

Limes are called "limones" in South America. This drink makes a refreshing change from our lemonade.

Serves 2-4

You will need:

chopping board

sharp knife

juice squeezer

measuring jug

small saucepan

wooden spoon

blender

Ingredients:

4 juicy limes

100g (3½oz) caster sugar

125ml (4fl oz) water

2 mugs crushed ice

What to do:

• Put the sugar and water in the saucepan. Bring to the boil, stirring until the sugar is dissolved. Take off the heat and leave to cool. Squeeze the limes.

• Put the sugar syrup, the lime juice and the crushed ice in the blender and blend until well mixed and slushy.

Molten Hot Chocolate Sauce

Some of the finest chocolate in the world comes from Peru, and this recipe is for special occasions only.

Serves 2-4

You will need:

medium, heavy-based saucepan

tablespoon

wooden spoon

Ingredients:

200g (7oz) dark chocolate

150ml (¼ pint) double cream

2 tbsp honey

50g (2oz) salted butter

What to do:

• Put all the ingredients in the saucepan. Stir over a low to medium heat until almost melted. Now add 3 tablespoons of boiling water and stir until completely smooth and glossy.

Pour the sauce over ice cream or poached pears. Or put it in a bowl and dip strawberries or marshmallows into it. P.B.

Lunch and Evening Meals

Nettle Soup

When it comes to asking anyone for advice on cooking, the Browns' next-door neighbour, Mr Curry, is normally the very last person I would have gone to. He is the meanest man on earth – always trying to get something for nothing, especially when it comes to a free meal. So what happened was all the more surprising.

I was in the garden one morning towards lunch time when I heard a lot of rustling on the other side of the fence and I was about to look through a knothole to see what was going on when he beat me to it.

"Spying on me again, bear!" he bellowed, poking his head over the fence.

"Oh, no, Mr Curry," I said. "I was worried you might have fallen over by mistake. Your garden is so full of nettles it would be an awful way to go."

To cut a long story short, I must have caught him on a good day. Instead of threatening to report me, he explained all about making soup out of nettles.

It was very interesting because apart from being free, nettles are full of vitamins and other essentials like iron. Turning them into soup makes for a very refreshing lunch-time snack or even the beginning to an evening meal.

Serves 2-4

You will need:

strong rubber gloves to protect you from being stung while you gather nettles

scissors

shopping bag to hold nettles

large saucepan with lid

chopping board

sharp knife

wooden spoon

measuring jug

hand blender (or liquidiser)

Ingredients:

enough nettles to fill the shopping bag loosely

50g (2oz) butter

1 medium onion

1 medium potato

1 litre (1¾ pints) chicken or vegetable stock

salt and pepper

3 tbsp crème fraîche (plus a little extra, to garnish)

parsley or chives

What to do:

- Wearing rubber gloves, gather the nettles, choosing the small, new leaves at the tops of the plants. Never pick nettles that have started flowering.

- Still wearing your rubber gloves, wash the nettles thoroughly.

- Remove the gloves and chop the onion. Melt the butter in the saucepan, add the chopped onion and cook slowly, with the lid on, until soft but not browned.

- Chop the potato and add to the pan, stirring it in with the onion and butter mixture.

- Put the gloves back on to pile in the nettles and then pour on the stock. Stir gently – you will find the nettles quickly wilt and sink down. At the same time they lose their sting.

- Bring to the boil, turn down the heat and simmer with the lid on for about 15 minutes, until the potato is soft and the nettles are tender.

- Taste, and add salt and pepper if needed.

- Purée the soup with a hand blender in the saucepan, or in batches, in a liquidiser.

- Stir in the crème fraîche and reheat the soup, but don't let it boil.

- When you serve it, add a swirl of crème fraîche, and a sprinkling of parsley or chopped chives.

If you want a more filling lunch to follow on from the nettle soup why not try…

Spicy Chicken Noodles

Serves 2-4

You will need:

bowl

chopping board

sharp knife

tablespoon

wok or frying pan

measuring jug

wooden spoon

What to do:

• Cook the noodles, following the instructions on the packet, and set aside. Measure out the sweetcorn and peas and leave them in a bowl to defrost.

• Cut the chicken into strips. Chop the spring onions.

Ingredients:

125g (4½oz) Chinese noodles, cooked (or ready to use)

75g (3oz) frozen sweetcorn kernels

75g (3oz) frozen peas

400g (14oz) chicken breast

4 spring onions

3 tbsp vegetable oil

2 tbsp mild curry paste (korma is ideal)

150ml (¼ pint) chicken stock

150ml (¼ pint) coconut milk

pinch of dried red chilli flakes

juice of ½ lime

- Heat the oil in the wok or frying pan. Add the spring onions and stir fry for about 2 minutes.

- Now add the chicken strips and stir and cook for 5 minutes.

- Add the curry paste, stock, coconut milk and chilli flakes. Stir well, bring it up to a simmer and let it cook for 10 minutes.

- Add the noodles, sweetcorn and peas, and cook everything for a further 3 minutes.

- Lastly, add the lime juice, give everything a final stir and serve up in bowls.

Rich Red Sauce

Pasta in its many forms is popular with all ages, but if you feel the need to spice it up a little, Mrs Bird recommends the following sauce:

Serves 2-4

You will need:

chopping board

sharp knife

medium saucepan

teaspoon

wooden spoon

wand blender or liquidiser

What to do:

- Cut the peppers in half and take out the seeds and the white membrane. Chop the peppers into fairly small pieces.

- Cut the tomatoes roughly in the tin with a knife and put them in the saucepan with the peppers. Fill the empty tin to about a quarter with water, swill it round, and add to the pan with the chilli flakes and sugar.

Ingredients:

2 medium/large red peppers

400g (14oz) tin tomatoes

good pinch dried red chilli flakes

1 level tsp caster sugar

salt and pepper

1 tbsp olive oil

• Stir, bring the mixture to a simmer and cook for about 30 minutes, stirring now and then, until the peppers are soft. Liquidise with a wand blender or liquidiser. Add salt and pepper to taste, together with the olive oil.

This sauce is delicious with any kind of pasta, especially with grated cheese on top. P. B.

Mrs Bird's Beef Stew with Dumplings

Beef Stew

Serves 4-6

You will need:

chopping board

sharp knife

large saucepan with lid

wooden spoon

tablespoon

large plate or bowl

measuring jug

mixing bowl

sieve

Ingredients:

700g (1lb 8oz) good quality braising steak

4 tbsp plain flour

4 tbsp oil or dripping

1 large onion

4 carrots

1¼ litres (2 pints) good beef stock

bay leaf

salt and pepper

What to do:

- Trim any extra fat off the beef and cut into walnut-sized chunks. Chop the onion finely and slice the carrots.

- Heat 3 tablespoons of oil or dripping in the saucepan.

- Dust the meat with 3 tablespoons of flour, half a teaspoon of salt and a few grinds of black pepper (a good way of doing this is to put the chunks of meat and the flour in a bag, hold tightly shut, and shake well).

- Fry the meat over quite a high heat – in batches, so that it browns rather than steams. As each batch is browned, take it out of the pan and put aside on a large plate or bowl.

- Turn the heat down and add the last tablespoon of oil or dripping. Add the onion and carrots and cook slowly, stirring now and then, until they are lightly browned at the edges.

- Sprinkle on the last tablespoon of flour and stir well for a minute or two.

- Add the stock, the bay leaf, the meat and any juices that have come out of it. Heat until it is just simmering, cover with the lid, and cook very gently for about an hour and a half, until the meat is tender.

Dumplings

Mrs Bird's dumplings are well known in the neighbourhood. Light and airy, they melt in the mouth and add tone to any beef stew. They can be prepared some twenty minutes or so before it is time to begin the meal.

Ingredients:

115g (4oz) self-raising flour

extra flour for your hands

55g (2oz) shredded suet

pinch of salt

What to do:

• Sift the flour and salt into the mixing bowl. Add the suet and mix in enough cold water (about 125ml/4fl oz) to make a light dough.

• Flour your hands. Take a lump of dough about the size of a walnut, roll it between your palms to make a ball, and drop it into the hot stew. Carry on until all the dough is used up or there is no room left for any more.

• Bring back to a simmer, put the lid on the saucepan, and cook for another 15-20 minutes.

MRS BIRD'S TIP:
Don't over work the kneading. The more pockets of air left in the mixture, the lighter they will be and as the air expands with the heat so the dumplings will rise to the surface. When this happens, give them another few minutes and serve.

Perfect Roast Potatoes

Another thing Mrs Bird is very proud of is her roast potatoes.

MRS BIRD'S SECRET:
Her potatoes have an extra lovely, thick, crispy outside to them because once they have been par-boiled and are waiting to be put in the fat, having first made sure they are cool enough to handle, she scores their surface with a fork. Sometimes she lets me do it for her. It isn't easy with paws, but it's well worth the trouble and it never fails.

Serves 4-6

You will need:

large roasting tin

chopping board

potato peeler

sharp knife

large saucepan

colander

oven gloves

large spoon

*measuring jug
(for the oil)*

Ingredients:

*1kg (2lb 4oz) floury potatoes.
Desireé, King Edward or
Maris Piper are good*

*80g (3½oz) goose or duck
fat (many people think these
make the best, crunchiest
roast potatoes). Healthy
alternatives are 80ml
(2¾fl oz) sunflower or
rapeseed oil*

salt

What to do:

- Preheat the oven to 200°C (400°F/Gas mark 6).
  Put the roasting tin inside to warm.

- Peel the potatoes and cut into similar-sized chunks.

- Place them in a large saucepan of cold water.
  Add a good sprinkle of salt and bring to the boil,
  then simmer for about 5-7 minutes.

- Drain in the colander, and leave for about 5 minutes
  to steam and dry out a little.

- Using oven gloves, take the roasting tin out of the
  oven and add the fat or oil. Put the tin back in the
  oven.

- Tip the potatoes back into the empty saucepan and
  give them a good shake to roughen up the edges.

- Now add them to the roasting tin and, with the
  spoon, turn them over in the sizzling fat to coat
  them. Space them out so they have room to brown.

- Put the tin back in the oven for about 45 minutes
  or just a little longer – until they are crisp and
  golden outside, and creamy and fluffy inside.

Sausages and Lentils

Serves 2-4

You will need:

large saucepan

tablespoon

wooden spoon

slotted spoon

chopping board

sharp knife

measuring jug

What to do:

• Heat the olive oil in the saucepan over a medium heat. Add the sausages and let them brown, turning from time to time.

• Take the sausages out of the pan with the slotted spoon.

Ingredients:

2 tbsp olive oil

500g (1lb 2oz) good quality sausages

1 medium onion

1 medium carrot

250g (9oz) lentils (puy or green)

1 litre (1¾ pints) chicken stock

1 bay leaf

salt and pepper

- Chop the onion and carrot and put in the saucepan. Cook, stirring occasionally, until slightly softened.

- Now add the lentils, stock and bay leaf. Put the sausages back in the saucepan, stir everything gently, and heat to a gentle simmer.

- Cook, with the lid on, for about half an hour – until the sausages are cooked and the lentils are soft but not mushy.

- Add salt and pepper to taste.

Chicken Paprika

"I wish, I wish, Mr Brown," said Mr Gruber when I asked him if he knew how to cook goulash. He was born in Hungary so I thought he was bound to know.

"All over the world, apart from Hungary itself, people think goulash is the Hungarian national dish. Centuries ago that was true. It was made with beef that had been cooked and then dried in the sun, and it was a favourite with the nomadic tribesmen tending their oxen. Sadly, the nearest you will find to the real thing these days is a watered-down version called 'gulyás levess' – meaning 'the soup of the cowboy'."

Instead, he gave me the recipe for a dish which many people feel has replaced goulash: Chicken Paprika.

Serves 4-6

You will need:

chopping board

sharp knife

teaspoon

tablespoon

measuring jug

saucepan with lid

wooden spoon

slotted spoon

large plate

Ingredients:

2 medium onions

125g (4½oz) mushrooms

400g (14oz) tin tomatoes

2 tbsp vegetable oil

1 chicken, jointed, or 8 chicken pieces

1 heaped tbsp paprika (hot or smoked, whatever you like) plus a little extra, for sprinkling

1 tsp caraway seeds

250ml (9fl oz) chicken stock

salt and pepper

150ml (¼ pint) soured cream

2 tbsp chopped parsley

What to do:

- Peel and chop the onions. Slice the mushrooms. Roughly chop the tomatoes in the tin.

- Heat the oil in the pan and fry the chicken pieces on all sides until they are golden (about 10 minutes).

- Take the chicken out of the pan with the slotted spoon and put on the plate.

- Put the onions in the pan (add a little more oil if needed). Add the paprika and caraway seeds, and cook, stirring with the wooden spoon, for about 2 minutes.

- Add the mushrooms and cook for another 3 minutes.

- Put in the tomatoes, the stock and the chicken. Bring to the boil and then turn down the heat, put the lid on and simmer gently for 40 minutes. Take the lid off and stir. If the sauce is too thin, take the lid off and simmer for another 10 minutes or so.

- Add salt and pepper to taste.

- Spoon the soured cream on top, swirling over the surface, and sprinkle on the parsley and a little paprika.

- Delicious served with buttered noodles, plain steamed or boiled rice, or potatoes.

Green Risotto

Serves 4-6

You will need:

chopping board

sharp knife

large saucepan

colander

food processor/liquidiser

large, heavy-based saucepan

wooden spoon

ladle

cheese grater

What to do:

- Wash the spinach and cut off any tough stalks.

- Put it, with the mint, in a saucepan of salted, boiling water for just a minute, to blanch. Drain, keeping the water.

- In the same water, cook the peas and drain. Liquidise the spinach, mint and peas, adding a little of the cooking water if necessary.

- Heat the vegetable stock. Grate the cheese.

- Chop the shallots or onion finely. Melt 50g (2oz) of the butter in the heavy-based saucepan over a medium heat, and cook the shallots or onion until soft. Add the rice and stir for a minute or two to absorb the onion-flavoured butter. You should hear the rice crackling when it is ready for the next stage.

Ingredients:

1kg (2lb 4oz) spinach

bunch of mint

250g (9oz) frozen peas

1 litre (1¾ pints) vegetable stock (bouillon powder is ideal for this)

100g (3½oz) Parmesan cheese

2 shallots or 1 medium onion

75g (3oz) butter

200g (7oz) risotto rice

salt and pepper

3 tbsp basil leaves (optional)

- Add 2 ladlefuls of stock and watch, stirring often, until it is absorbed into the rice. Carry on, a ladleful at a time, until the rice is almost completely soft but the risotto is still creamy. This should take about 20 minutes.

- Now stir in the spinach, mint and pea purée, the rest of the butter and half the Parmesan cheese. Add salt and pepper to taste, and basil leaves if you have them.

- Serve with the rest of the grated Parmesan.

fish in Paper Parcels

Serves 4

You will need:

4 sheets of baking parchment paper (1 for each person)

pencil

scissors

tablespoon

chopping board

sharp knife

What to do:

- Preheat the oven to 220°C (425°F/Gas mark 7).

- Fold the sheets of parchment in half lengthwise. Put a fillet of fish on top of each, near the fold, and draw a semi-circle round it, leaving a margin of at least 5cm (2in) all round. Take the fish off, cut out the shape and open into a circle.

- Put a fillet of fish on the right-hand side of each circle. Season with salt and pepper.

Ingredients:

4 fillets of fish (sole/ haddock/salmon – whatever you like)

salt and pepper

olive oil

lemon juice

4 tbsp chopped herbs: chervil, parsley, chives, or dill

• Sprinkle on a tablespoon of olive oil and a good squeeze of lemon juice.

• Now add a tablespoon or so of chopped herbs.

• Fold the papers over and seal by rolling and crimping the edges, overlapping as you go. It's important that there are no gaps.

• Put in the middle of the oven for about 15 minutes (or up to 25 minutes for a really thick fillet) until the parcels are puffed up and golden.

• Serve on a plate, in the paper. (It is fun to open the parcels at the table and smell the juices.)

Puddings

Apple Snow

This is one of my favourite puddings. It is simple, fresh and clean-tasting – just what you need if you have had one too many marmalade sandwiches. Mrs Bird says that when you are whisking egg whites, a squeeze of lemon juice helps to make them lovely and stiff.

Apple Snow

Serves 4-6

You will need:

chopping board

sharp knife

vegetable peeler

large saucepan

tablespoon

wooden spoon

sieve or blender

large bowl

electric hand whisk

large metal spoon

Ingredients:

900g (2lb) cooking apples

75g (3oz) caster sugar

3 egg whites

What to do:

- Peel the apples, cut into quarters and take out the cores. Cut into chunks.

- Put in the saucepan with the sugar and 2 tablespoons of water. Stir well with the wooden spoon. Cook over a low to medium heat, stirring occasionally, until the apples are soft.

- Purée the apples in a blender (or push through a sieve). Leave to cool.

- In the large bowl, beat the egg whites until they are stiff.

- With the large metal spoon, fold the egg whites into the apple purée. Chill in the fridge for 1-2 hours.

- Serve in bowls with chilled pouring cream.

floating Islands

Jonathan and Judy's favourite dessert is floating islands. I expect it's because they don't often have it at school. When I suggested that to Jonathan he gave a hollow laugh. "The word is never!" he said.

Serves 6

You will need:

measuring jug

wide, shallow saucepan

large saucepan

chopping board

sharp knife

large bowl

sieve

electric hand whisk

tablespoon

large spoon

slotted spoon

small, heavy-based saucepan

clean tea towel

dinner plate

What to do:

• Pour the milk into the wide, shallow saucepan. Split open the vanilla pods, scrape out the seeds and add both the pods and the seeds to the milk. Bring to a simmer, take off the heat and leave to infuse.

• Whisk 3 egg whites with a pinch of salt until firm. Still whisking, add 120g (4oz) of the caster sugar, a spoonful at a time, until the mixture becomes a glossy meringue.

Ingredients:

1¼ litres (2 pints) whole milk

2 vanilla pods

3 egg whites

4 egg yolks

pinch of salt

165g (6oz) caster sugar

110g (4oz) granulated sugar

- Bring the milk back to a simmer in the pan. Gently place 6 large spoonfuls of meringue into the milk. Poach for 4 minutes, turn over and poach for another 4 minutes.

- Gently lift the islands on to a plate lined with a clean tea towel to drain. Heat 500ml (18fl oz) of the vanilla milk (strained through a sieve) in the large saucepan. In a large bowl, whisk the 4 egg yolks with the remaining 45g (1½oz) caster sugar and add the hot milk, whisking all the time.

- Sieve the mixture into the rinsed out saucepan and stir over a low to medium heat until it is thick enough to coat the back of a spoon. Leave to cool and then chill. (This is the custard for later.)

- For the caramel, put the granulated sugar in the small saucepan with 3 tablespoons of water. Bring to a simmer, then take off the heat and swirl the pan until the sugar has dissolved and the liquid is clear. Put back on a medium to high heat and bring to the boil, swirling the pan occasionally until the syrup is caramel coloured.

- Spoon some custard on each serving plate, top with a poached meringue island and drizzle with caramel.

Huffkins

Mrs Bird was born in Kent in the days when it was known as "The Garden of England". During the spring, the countryside used to be awash with blossom from thousands of fruit trees, and after the fruit had all been harvested the occasion was celebrated by the baking of tarts known as huffkins.

Makes 12 huffkins

You will need:

2 large mixing bowls

measuring jug

teaspoon

sieve

saucepan

wooden spoon

large baking tray

What to do:

- Sift the flour into the bowl. Rub the butter into the flour until it looks like breadcrumbs. Add the salt and sugar. Leave in a warm place for 5 minutes.

- Pour the milk and water into the saucepan and heat until just warm.

- Crumble the yeast into the liquid and stir until blended. Pour the liquid on to the flour mixture and mix well.

Ingredients:

500g (1lb 2oz) plain flour

50g (2oz) butter

pinch of salt

2 tsp sugar

12g (½oz) fresh yeast, or 7g (¼oz) dried

120ml (4fl oz) milk

120ml (4fl oz) water

cherries or jam for the filling

- Put the dough on to a floured surface and knead until smooth. Put in a clean bowl and leave in a warm place for an hour to let the huffkins rise.

- Preheat oven to 220°C (425°F/Gas mark 7). Lightly grease the baking tray.

- Divide the dough into 12 pieces. Roll into balls and put them on the baking tray, flattening them slightly. With your finger (or paw), make a hole in the middle of each one. Leave to rise for 20 minutes, then bake for 20 minutes.

- Fill the holes with cherries or jam.

...or marmalade! P. B.

Bread and Butter Pudding with Marmalade

Bread and butter pudding with marmalade is my favourite, and luckily the rest of the family like it too. Jonathan calls it my marmalade sandwich pudding! But a word of warning: Mrs Bird says you can never improve on a dish which uses the best of ingredients, and this is a case in point. Don't even consider using a loaf of ready-sliced bread.

Bread and Butter Pudding with Marmalade

Serves 4-6

You will need:

chopping board

bread knife

round-bladed knife, for spreading

teaspoon

shallow ovenproof dish, about 20 x 30 x 5cm (8 x 12 x 12in)

bowl

tablespoon

measuring jug

whisk

Ingredients:

6 slices white bread, cut from a large loaf

75g (3oz) butter, soft enough to spread

3 heaped tbsp orange marmalade

3 large eggs

500ml (18fl oz) milk

50g (2oz) caster sugar

1 tsp vanilla extract

2 tbsp demerara sugar

What to do:

- Preheat the oven to 180°C (350°F/Gas mark 4).

- Spread 3 slices of the bread with butter, then marmalade, and top with the other 3 slices. Spread some butter on top of each sandwich and cut each one into 4.

- Lay the squares, buttered side up, slightly overlapping, in a buttered, ovenproof dish.

- Whisk the eggs, milk, caster sugar and vanilla extract together and pour over the dish. Let it stand for about half an hour, to allow the mixture to soak in.

- Sprinkle the demerara sugar over the surface.

- Bake for about 45 minutes, until it is puffed up and the top is golden.

- Serve with cream or ice cream.

Pancakes

Pancakes are always popular, but a lot of people fight shy of making them, so here is Mrs Bird's recipe.

Makes 12-14 pancakes

You will need:

mixing bowl

sieve

tablespoon

measuring jug

whisk (electric or hand)

frying pan

fish slice

large plate

clean tea towel

Ingredients:

125g (4½oz) plain flour

2 large eggs

200ml (7fl oz) whole milk

90ml (3fl oz) water

2 tbsp melted butter

butter, for cooking the pancakes

What to do:

- Sift the flour into the bowl and hollow out a well in the centre with the tablespoon.

- Break the eggs into the well and, with the whisk, begin to mix in the flour. Add the milk and water from the jug, gradually, whisking as you go, until the mixture is smooth. Now melt the butter in the pan, pour into the mixture and whisk in.

- Put the pan over a medium heat and add a knob of butter, coating the base. Pour 2 tablespoons of batter into the pan, tipping it so the base is covered. Cook for about 1 minute until bubbles appear on the surface. Then flip over with the fish slice (or toss, if you are brave) and heat on the other side until just cooked through.

- As you make the pancakes, pile them on a plate and cover them with the tea towel to keep them warm and soft.

MRS BIRD'S TIP:
Serve simply with sugar and
lemon juice. Some people like
jam, or why not try golden syrup
and ice cream for a change?

Summer Holidays

Summer is a time for picnics and by general agreement, once Paddington had completed his cookery course in Mrs Bird's kitchen, the rest of the family turned to him for advice.

As usual he was put in charge of making the sandwiches, and although calls soon went out for more jars of marmalade (a picnic wouldn't have been the same without them) other goodies began to appear.

"Paddington's a dab hand at making sandwiches these days," whispered Jonathan, busying himself with some hot dogs.

"He's had plenty of practice over the years," murmured Judy, carefully cutting some hard-boiled eggs in two.

"I know," said Jonathan, "but apart from marmalade, there's scrambled egg with mayonnaise, cream cheese, peanut butter, ham… He'll be opening a restaurant soon if we don't watch out."

Packing the heated hot dogs and their liquid into a wide-necked Thermos flask kept for the purpose, he began looking for the ketchup.

"Pass me a lemon," said Judy. "I've filled the egg shells with a mixture of tuna, egg, and mayonnaise. All it needs now is a squeeze of lemon and we can stick the two halves together and pack them in egg boxes for safe keeping."

Tzatziki

"Has anyone seen the recipe for tzatziki?" said Judy.

"I have it," called Mrs Brown. "I'll read it out to you if you like."

"I bet she can't even spell it," said Jonathan, "let alone make it."

"Just for that," said Judy, "you can see if there are any falafels left in the fridge. Tzatziki and falafels are great together."

I think this is an ideal do-it-yourself dish because if I tried to order it in a restaurant I wouldn't know how to pronounce it. Who knows what I might get! P. B.

Serves 2-4

You will need:

chopping board

sharp knife

vegetable peeler

teaspoon

colander

bowl

kitchen paper

tablespoon

Ingredients:

1 cucumber

salt

350g (12oz) Greek yogurt

2 tbsp lemon juice

2 cloves garlic

3 tbsp chopped mint

What to do:

- Peel the cucumber. Cut in half lengthwise and scoop out the seeds with the teaspoon.

- Chop the cucumber, put it in the colander, sprinkle with salt and leave for an hour or so to drain off some of its juices.

- Rinse the cucumber and pat dry with kitchen paper. Put it in a clean bowl and add the yogurt.

- Chop the garlic finely. Add the mint and garlic to the bowl.

- Pour on the lemon juice and mix everything well. Decant into a container with a lid.

- Pack some vegetable strips (cucumber, carrot, pepper) and some pitta bread or Italian bread, for dipping.

Marmalade Chicken Drumsticks

Meanwhile, in a quiet part of the kitchen, unperturbed by all the fuss going on around her, Mrs Bird was preparing one of Paddington's favourites:

Makes 10

You will need:

baking tray

kitchen foil

tablespoon

small saucepan

wooden spoon

sharp knife

grater

Ingredients:

10 chicken drumsticks

5 tbsp marmalade (not too chunky – fine cut, or shredless is even better)

1 tbsp Worcestershire sauce

zest and juice of ½ an orange

What to do:

- Preheat oven to 190°C (375°F/Gas mark 5).

- Line a baking tray with foil (this makes it much easier to clean).

- Put the marmalade, Worcestershire sauce, orange zest and juice in the saucepan.

- Heat gently, stirring with the wooden spoon, until it is all well mixed.

- Arrange the chicken drumsticks on the baking sheet, and pour over the marmalade mixture, coating each one.

- Put in the oven and cook for about 45 minutes. You know they are ready when you stick a sharp knife into a drumstick and the juices come out clear.

- Leave to cool, pack in a container, and keep in the fridge until you set off.

"I've packed some handwipes," she called, as the others left. "I have a feeling you may need them."

The sun shone that day and everyone voted it was the best picnic they'd had since the last one.

On days when the sun doesn't shine – or, worse still … it begins to rain – all is not lost. At the very worst Jonathan, Judy and Paddington go without supper and have a "midnight feast" in his bedroom instead; which, it has to be said, usually starts around half past eight and finishes long before the clock in the hall strikes twelve.

But on one such day towards the end of the holiday when the clouds looked full of rain and they had given up all hope of a picnic, Mr and Mrs Brown packed everything into the boot of the car and instead of waiting for the rain to make up its mind, drove out of London in the hope of finding better weather.

Blackberry and Apple Crumble

Their journey paid off, for after a while the sun broke through a gap in the clouds and gradually the countryside came to life again.

When Mr Brown pulled into a picnic area to study the map, it was Jonathan who spotted it first; a hedgerow which was positively festooned with the first of the season's blackberries.

Paddington was most surprised. "I've never seen a blackberry before!" he exclaimed. "I don't think we had them in Darkest Peru."

"Wait until you taste them," said Judy. "I know what's going to be on the menu tonight when Mrs Bird sees them – blackberry and apple crumble."

Mr Brown fished a walking stick out of the boot, and using the crook to capture the higher branches where the best fruit was clustered (much to the disgust of the birds) they soon had all they needed.

"Right," said Mrs Bird, when she saw their haul. "I shall need your help, Paddington."

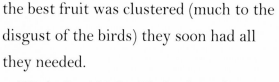

Blackberry and Apple Crumble

Serves 4-6

You will need:

chopping board

sharp knife

potato peeler

ovenproof dish about 20 x 30cm & 5cm deep (8 x 12in & 2in deep)

mixing bowl

sieve

tablespoon

Ingredients:

500g (1lb 2oz) cooking apples

250g (9oz) blackberries

55g (2oz) caster sugar

200g (7oz) plain flour

100g (3½oz) unsalted, cold butter, cut into cubes

125g (4½oz) demerara sugar

What to do:

- Preheat the oven to 200°C (400°F/Gas mark 6).

- Peel and core the apples and cut into large chunks. Wash the blackberries and place all the fruit in the ovenproof dish.

- Add the caster sugar, and mix it through the fruit with your hands to spread it about.

- To make the crumble, sieve the flour into the mixing bowl and add the butter. Rub the butter into the flour with your fingertips, until the mixture looks like breadcrumbs. Stir in the demerara sugar.

- Spread the crumble mixture over the fruit in the dish and pat it down so there are no bald patches.

- Bake for 35-40 minutes, until the top is golden brown and there are purple juices bubbling at the edges.

- Leave for 10 minutes before dishing up. Serve with cream, crème fraîche or ice cream.

Paddington's Christmas Birthday Party

As everyone knows, bears have two birthdays a year – just like the Queen of England; or so Paddington assured the Browns soon after he arrived in London. And since he was an honourable bear, no one had any cause to doubt him.

But as anyone whose birthday happens to fall on Christmas Day will tell you, it is not the best arrangement in the world.

That being so, the Browns try to lessen the problem by celebrating Paddington's winter birthday with a party during Jonathan and Judy's last half-term holiday of the year.

It went without saying that Mr Gruber had a standing invitation, and somehow or other Mr Curry usually managed to worm his way in, but because Paddington was such a well-known figure in the neighbourhood, a number of small children were usually invited to join in too.

There was so much to do, Paddington had to forgo his elevenses with Mr Gruber for the next day or two, but as his friend said, "Needs must, Mr Brown. It's all in a good cause."

Sticky Marmalade Sausages

Serves 4-6

You will need:

shallow ovenproof dish

mixing bowl

tablespoon

teaspoon

scissors or sharp knife

Ingredients:

500g (1lb 2oz) good quality sausages

4 tbsp marmalade (fine shred is best)

2 tsp mustard – smooth or grainy

2 tbsp orange juice

What to do:

- Preheat the oven to 190°C (375°F/Gas mark 5).

- Separate the sausages.

- In the bowl, mix together the marmalade, the mustard and the orange juice.

- Making sure your hands are clean, put the sausages in the ovenproof dish and coat with the marmalade mixture.

- Cook for 30 minutes, turning and basting half way through.

MRS BIRD'S TIP:
Lining your cooking dish with foil makes it much easier to clean.

Gingerbread Bears

The first items to prepare in advance were gingerbread bears, to act as presents for the smaller guests.

Makes 8-10 bears

You will need:

large baking tray

teaspoon

tablespoon

sieve

mixing bowl

round-bladed knife

rolling pin

oven gloves

wire cooling rack

bear-shaped biscuit cutter

Ingredients:

200g (7oz) self-raising flour

pinch of salt

2 level tsp ground ginger

1 level tsp ground cinnamon

100g (3½oz) unsalted butter

75g (3oz) soft brown sugar

3 tbsp milk

What to do:

- Place a shelf just above the centre of the oven and preheat to 200°C/400°F/Gas mark 6.

- Lightly grease the baking tray.

- Sift the flour, salt, ginger and cinnamon through the sieve into the mixing bowl.

- Add the butter and cut it into the dry mixture with the round-bladed knife to make tiny pieces. Now rub it in with your fingertips until the mixture looks like breadcrumbs. Add the sugar.

- Mix in the milk with the knife and gather it all together with your hands to make a fairly stiff dough.

- Put on to a surface dusted with flour and shape into a ball.

- Roll out fairly thinly with a floured rolling pin. Cut out bears with the biscuit cutter.

- Gather together the trimmings, re-roll and cut out more bears. Place them on the greased tray.

Decorating your bears:

You will need:

luggage labels

scissors

black felt-tip pen

piping bag or icing syringe

Ingredients:

125g (4½oz) icing sugar

edible gold or silver balls or currants

1 tbsp tepid water (from the kettle)

What to do:

- Push 3 gold or silver balls, or currants, into the front of the bears, for buttons.

- Bake for 10-15 minutes or until the bears are golden brown.

- Leave the tray to stand for 10 minutes before carefully lifting off the bears on to a wire rack to cool.

- Mix icing sugar with a little water to make white icing. Put it in a piping bag or syringe.

- When the bears are quite cold, ice on eyes, noses and mouths, as shown.

Trim the luggage labels with the scissors to make them smaller. Write "for" and a guest's name on each label and then tie round the bears' necks.

FOR JUDITH

Sponge Birthday Cake

The next important item which can be prepared in advance is a sponge birthday cake.

You Will Need:

mixing bowl

sieve

teaspoon

tablespoon

electric hand mixer (or wooden spoon)

2 x 20cm (8in) sandwich tins, lightly greased, bases lined with baking parchment

palette knife

wire rack

sharp knife

large plate, for serving

birthday candles

Ingredients:

175g (6oz) self-raising flour

1 rounded tsp baking powder

3 large eggs

175g (6oz) caster sugar

175g (6oz) unsalted, softened butter

½ tsp vanilla extract

2 tbsp milk

What to do:

- Preheat oven to 180°C (350°F/Gas mark 4).

- Sift the flour and baking powder into the mixing bowl, holding the sieve high to make sure that lots of air gets in. Now add all the other cake ingredients to the bowl.

- Using the electric hand mixer, beat until the mixture is really whipped and smooth. If you don't have an electric mixer, use a wooden spoon. You will have to beat hard, and it will take longer, but it will work. You want a mixture which drops softly off the spoon. Divide the cake mix between the two tins and level off the tops with the palette knife.

- Place on the middle shelf of the oven for 30 minutes. Don't open the door while they are cooking, or the cakes may collapse.

- Test to see if the cakes are ready by pressing very lightly on the middle of one with a finger. If the sponge springs back, the cakes are ready.

- Take the tins out of the oven and leave for about 10 minutes before turning the cakes out on to the wire rack. Leave them to get completely cold and carefully peel off the paper from the bottoms before filling.

Filling:

Ingredients:

3 tbsp strawberry jam

punnet of strawberries

1 small pot double cream

icing sugar (for the top)

What to do:

- Place one sponge on the serving plate. Spread the jam over the top.

- Now put the strawberries on top of the jam, cutting any large ones in half.

- Whip the cream until it's thick but still soft, and dollop on top of the strawberries, spreading lightly to cover them.

- Place the other sponge on top. Finish by sifting over a fine dusting of icing sugar.

MRS BIRD'S TIP:
For the filling, instead of strawberries, you can use raspberry jam and raspberries.

Cupcakes

Makes 12 cupcakes

You will need:

12-bun muffin tray, lined with 12 cupcake paper cases

mixing bowl

tablespoon

teaspoon

hand mixer

spatula

wire rack

Ingredients:

125g (4½oz) unsalted butter, softened

125g (4½oz) caster sugar

2 large eggs

125g (4½oz) self-raising flour

1 tsp baking powder

1 tsp vanilla extract

2 tbsp milk

What to do:

• Preheat oven to 180°C (350°F/Gas mark 4).

• Place all the ingredients in the mixing bowl. Whizz with the mixer until everything is blended and smooth.

• Spoon the mixture into the paper cases. Use a spatula to scrape up all the mixture from the bowl, trying to give each case an equal amount.

• Put the tray in the oven and bake for 15-20 minutes, until the cakes are cooked and golden brown.

• Remove the cakes from the tray and leave on the wire rack to cool.

To ice:

You will need:

bowl

teaspoon

round-bladed knife

Ingredients:

250g (9oz) icing sugar

water, lemon juice or orange juice

What to do:

• Put the icing sugar in the bowl and, gradually – by the teaspoon – add water, lemon or orange juice, mixing with the knife until you get the right consistency: not too thick or thin.

• When the cupcakes are cold, ice them with the knife.

Mrs Bird's suggestions for toppings:

Add a few drops of food colouring to the icing. (Put a little of the icing in a mug if you want to use different colours and add the colour a drop at a time.)

Decorate with glacé cherries, crystallised petals or gold or silver balls.

For Paddington cupcakes, cut a footprint shape out of paper. Holding the paper stencil over the cupcake, sift cocoa powder lightly over it while the icing is still wet.

Brown Bread Ice Cream

Serves 2-4

You will need:

baking tray

wooden spoon

mixing bowl

another bowl

electric hand whisk

large spoon, to mix

container or serving dish for freezing

What to do:

• Preheat oven to 200°C (400°F/Gas mark 6).

• Mix the breadcrumbs with half the sugar and spread over the baking tray. Put in the oven for about 10-12 minutes, looking at the crumbs occasionally and mixing them about a bit with the wooden spoon. Watch that they don't burn – you want them crispy and just browned. Take them out of the oven, and leave to cool.

• Beat both the single and the double cream together until thick and floppy. Add the rest of the sugar and the egg yolks and beat until just melted through.

• Tip in the breadcrumbs and mix them through thoroughly.

Ingredients:

175g (6oz) brown breadcrumbs (the easiest way to make these is to whizz them up in a food processor)

125g (4½oz) soft brown sugar

300ml (10fl oz) double cream

300ml (10fl oz) single cream

2 eggs, separated

- Clean the whisk, and whip the egg whites in the other bowl until stiff. Fold them through the mixture.

- Pour the ice cream mix into your container or serving dish and put in the freezer for several hours, or overnight.

- This ice cream does not need to be churned or stirred while it's freezing. Take it out of the freezer and put in the fridge half an hour before serving, to let it soften a little.

- Serve on its own, or with fruit. (Delicious with strawberries!)

Popcorn

Serves 2-4

You will need:

large saucepan with lid

tablespoon

large bowl

small saucepan

wooden spoon

Ingredients:

2 tbsp vegetable oil

60g (2½oz) popping corn

50g (2oz) butter (optional)

food colouring (optional)

What to do:

- Put 2 tablespoons of vegetable oil in a saucepan. Add the popcorn (just enough to cover the bottom of the pan). Put the lid on the pan and cook on a high heat, shaking the pan hard to coat every kernel with oil.

- Listen to what is happening inside the pan. When the popping has almost stopped, take the pan off the heat. Wait until all the popping has stopped. Now pour the popcorn into the bowl.

- Of course, you can eat the popcorn just as it is. To make brilliant, coloured popcorn, heat the butter gently in the small saucepan until just melted. Add a drop or two of food colouring (start with the tiniest amount – it is very concentrated), stir into the butter, and pour over the popcorn in the bowl. Mix well – it will pick up the colour unevenly for an eye-catching marbled effect.

fizzy Jellies

Put some sparkle
in your party!

Serves 2-4

You will need:

measuring jug

wooden spoon

*small glass dishes, glasses,
or teacups, to serve*

Ingredients:

*1 block of jelly, whatever
flavour you like*

*420ml (15fl oz) fizzy
lemonade (you can use
sugar-free lemonade)*

What to do:

- Before you start, make sure the lemonade is as cold
  as possible – from the fridge, or put it in the freezer
  for half an hour.

- Break up the jelly into squares and put it in the
  measuring jug. Pour on hot water (from a kettle)
  to the 150ml (¼ pint) mark, and stir until it's
  dissolved. Leave to cool (but don't let it begin to set).

- Now pour in lemonade to make the liquid up to
  570ml (1 pint) – slowly, down the side of the jug, to
  keep all the bubbles in.

- Pour into your chosen containers and leave to set in
  the fridge for at least 4 hours.

85

Apple Tarts

Use good quality ready-made puff pastry (check there is butter in it) and these are quick, simple to make, and very, very tasty.

Makes 4 tarts

You will need:

large baking tray

rolling pin

chopping board

sharp knife

13cm (5in) plate or saucer

fork

vegetable peeler

small saucepan

pastry brush

tablespoon

wooden spoon

What to do:

- Preheat the oven to 200°C (400°F/Gas mark 6). Lightly grease the baking tray.

- On a floured surface, roll out the pastry thinly, to about 2mm (⅛in).

- Cut round the plate (or saucer) to make 4 pastry circles.

- Put the circles on the baking tray. Prick them all over with a fork (this stops them puffing up).

- Peel, core and quarter the apples. Cut them into thin slices and arrange on top of the pastry circles so they overlap. Finish off with 2 slices in the middle of each tart.

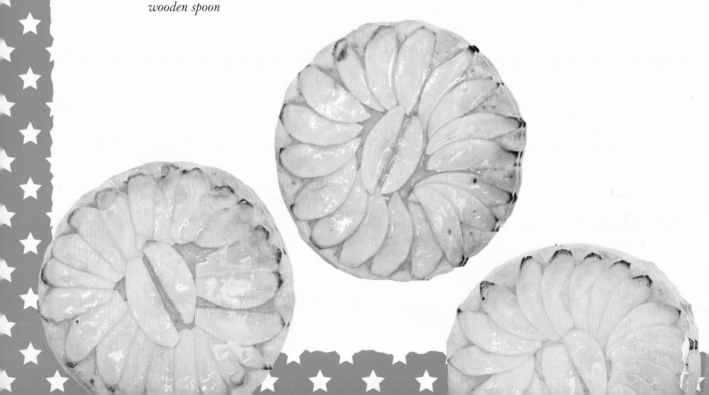

Ingredients:

250g (9oz) ready-made puff pastry

flour, for rolling out

4 eating apples (Braeburn or Granny Smith are good)

20g (¾oz) unsalted butter

2 tbsp caster sugar

½ jar apricot jam

1 tbsp lemon juice

- Melt the butter in a pan and brush all over the tarts. Cover each one with a fine sprinkling of caster sugar.

- Bake for 10-15 minutes, until the pastry is cooked. Any unused pastry can be wrapped in clingfilm and kept in the fridge for future use.

- Melt the apricot jam gently in the saucepan, stirring with the wooden spoon (if it is very chunky, sieve it first). Add the lemon juice and stir well. While it is still warm, brush the melted jam over the surface of the tarts.

- Serve warm – ideally with vanilla ice cream.

Bear-faced Party Pizzas

Last but not least to prepare because they need to be hot for the start of the party, are bear-faced party pizzas.

Makes 4 pizzas

You will need:

2 large baking sheets

large bowl

sieve

teaspoon

tablespoon

measuring jug

clean tea towel

chopping board

sharp knife

rolling pin

wooden spoon

medium saucepan

Ingredients:

Pizza dough:

350g (12oz) strong white bread flour

7g (¼oz) sachet instant dried yeast

1 tsp salt

200ml (7fl oz) warm water (from the kettle)

1½ tbsp olive oil

What to do:

• Sift the flour into the bowl and add the yeast and salt. Add the water and olive oil and mix until you have a dough which leaves the sides of the bowl cleanly (start off with the tablespoon, and then go in with your hands).

• Put on a floured surface and knead for 10 minutes (press down on the lump of dough with the heel of your hand, stretch it out with your other hand, fold it over, turn it round and repeat). Put the dough back in the bowl, cover with the clean tea towel and leave somewhere warm (like an airing cupboard) for about 1½ hours, until it has doubled in size.

Sauce:

2 shallots or 1 medium onion

400g (14oz) tin chopped tomatoes

2 tbsp olive oil, and a little extra for greasing

1 level tsp sugar

herbs: 1 tsp chopped thyme or rosemary (or 2 tbsp fresh basil, added at the end)

pinch salt and pepper

Topping:

4 large field mushrooms

8 pitted black olives

- To make the sauce, chop the shallots or onion. Heat the olive oil in the saucepan over a medium heat, add the shallots or onion and cook, stirring now and then, until soft. Add the tomatoes, sugar, herbs, salt and pepper, and stir. Turn down the heat and simmer for about 20 minutes, until thickened.

- Preheat the oven to 220°C (425°F/Gas mark 7).

- Take the dough out of the bowl and put on a floured surface.

- Knead again for 5 minutes. Cut it into 4 pieces.

- Flour the rolling pin and roll the pieces of dough into circles about 17cm (7in) in diameter.

- Grease the baking sheets with a little oil. Put the rounds of dough on the sheets and spread with the sauce.

- Now add the face. Cut ears from the dark underside of the mushrooms, with the gills going upwards. The noses are ovals cut from the tops. Cut olives in half for eyes. Slice an olive into 3 thin strips to make a mouth. Drizzle the faces with a little olive oil and smooth some over the noses to make them shine.

- Place in the oven and cook for 15-20 minutes until the sauce is just bubbling.

After most of the guests had left it was noticeable that Paddington had disappeared. No amount of calling his name received an answer. But then, nobody thought of looking in the kitchen.

Just as they were all getting worried that he might have got locked out of the house by mistake, the door to the living room opened and Paddington entered waving a sparkler with one paw and carrying a large plate laden with cheese straws in the other. They were piping hot from the oven.

Mr Gruber was the first to recover. "Bravo, Mr Brown," he said. "Bravo!"

"Not bad," said Mr Curry grudgingly, as he grabbed a handful. "Not bad at all."

"How ever did you make them?" asked Mrs Brown, when everyone else had settled down. "They are perfectly delicious. You must give us the recipe."

"Well," said Paddington. He consulted a piece of paper he had in his duffle coat pocket.

"You will need some of Mrs Bird's leftover pastry, some Cheddar cheese, a cheese grater…" The rest was drowned in laughter.

"Ask a silly question," said Mrs Brown.

"But this pattern round the edge," broke in Mr Brown, holding up a half-eaten piece of pastry. "It's most unusual. How did you do that?"

"It was all done by paw," said Paddington. "Bears' claws come in useful in an emergency."

Mr Brown looked for a moment as though he wished he hadn't asked.

"It's what is known as 'The Finishing Touch'," said Mrs Bird firmly. "All the best chefs have one, don't they, Paddington? It's what separates the bears from the boys. And if you ask me, this bear has passed his test with flying colours."

"Speech!" cried someone. It sounded like Mr Gruber.

Paddington hid his embarrassment under a loud, "Mmmmmmm. I'm afraid I can't for the moment," he announced. "I'm having trouble with my straws!"

List of Recipes

Breakfast

Scrambled Eggs

Marmalade

Tropical Pineapple Smoothie

Strawberry Bounce Smoothie

Paddington's Bargain Splurge Smoothie

Blueberry Muffins

Elevenses

Real Hot Chocolate

Iced Buns

Croque Monsieur

Portobello Road

Falafels

Roasted Pumpkin Soup

Rosted Pumpkin and Couscous Salad

Stuffed Baked Potatoes

Sweetcorn Fritters

Guacamole

Aunt Lucy's Corner

Sweet Potato Mash

Frozen Limonada

Molten Hot Chocolate Sauce

Lunch and Dinner Dishes

Nettle Soup
Spicy Chicken Noodles
Rich Red Sauce
Mrs Bird's Beef Stew with Dumplings
Perfect Roast Potatoes
Sausages and Lentils
Chicken Paprika
Green Risotto
Fish in Paper Parcels

Puddings

Apple Snow
Floating Islands
Huffkins
Bread and Butter Pudding with Marmalade
Pancakes

Summer Holidays

Tzatziki
Marmalade Chicken Drumsticks
Blackberry and Apple Crumble

Paddington's Christmas Birthday Party

Sticky Marmalade Sausages
Gingerbread Bears
Sponge Birthday Cake
Cupcakes
Brown Bread Ice Cream
Popcorn
Fizzy Jellies
Apple Tarts
Bear-Faced Party Pizzas

Index

A

apple
    apple snow 56-57
    apple tarts 86-87
    blackberry and apple crumble 72-73

B

bear-faced party pizzas 88-89
beef stew with dumplings, Mrs Bird's
    44-45
blackberry and apple crumble 72-73
blueberry muffins 18-19
bread
    bread and butter pudding with
        marmalade 62-63
    brown bread ice cream 82-83
    croque monsieur 24-25
    buns, iced 22-23

C

cake
    blueberry muffins 18-19
    cupcakes 80-81
    iced buns 22-23
    sponge birthday cake 78-79
cheese
    croque monsieur 24-25
    stuffed baked potatoes 30-31
chocolate
    molten hot chocolate sauce 37
    real hot chocolate 20-21
chicken
    chicken paprika 50-51
    marmalade chicken drumsticks
       70
    spicy chicken noodles 40-41

croque monsieur 24-25
cupcakes 80-81

D

dips
    guacamole 33
    tzatziki 68-69
drinks
    frozen limonada 36
    real hot chocolate 20-21
dumplings 45

E

eggs, scrambled 11

F

falafels 27
fish in paper parcels 54-55
fizzy jellies 85
floating islands 58-59
fritters, sweetcorn 32
frozen limonada 36
fruit
    apple snow 56-57
    apple tarts 86-87
    blackberry and apple crumble 72-73
    blueberry muffins 18-19
    frozen limonada 36
    tropical pineapple smoothie 16
    strawberry bounce smoothie 16
    Paddington's bargain splurge
       smoothie 17

G

green risotto 52-53
gingerbread bears 76-77
guacamole 33